Washington Monument

Lori Dittmer

Creative Education • Creative Paperbacks

National Mall
Washington, D.C.

Welcome to the Washington **Monument**! It is part of the National Mall and Memorial Parks in Washington, D.C. It stands between the United States Capitol and the Lincoln Memorial.

The Washington Monument was finished in 1884. At that time, it was the tallest building in the world. It is still the tallest structure in the city.

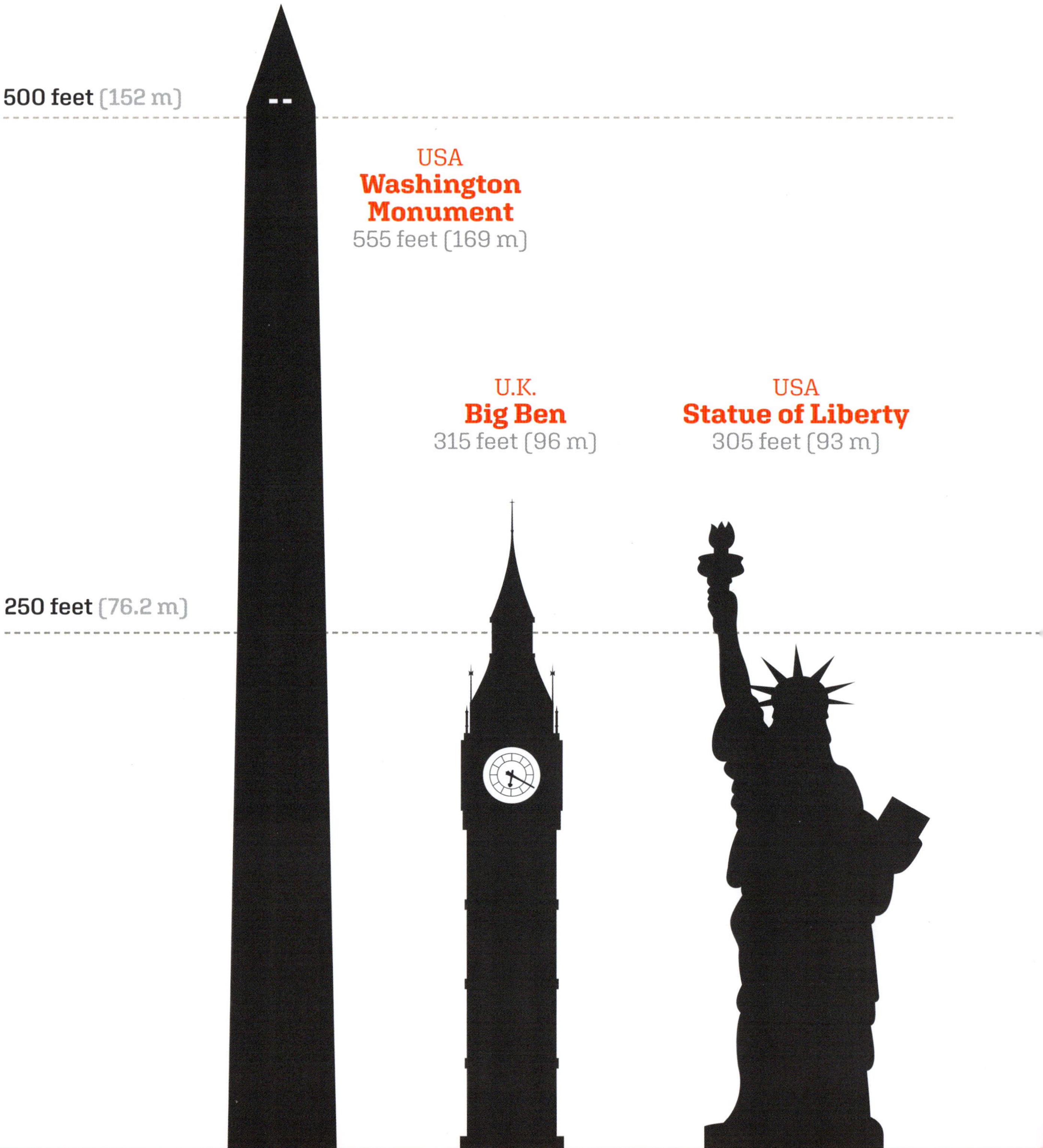

500 feet (152 m)
USA
Washington Monument
555 feet (169 m)
U.K.
Big Ben
315 feet (96 m)
USA
Statue of Liberty
305 feet (93 m)
250 feet (76.2 m)

How tall is the **Washington Monument?**

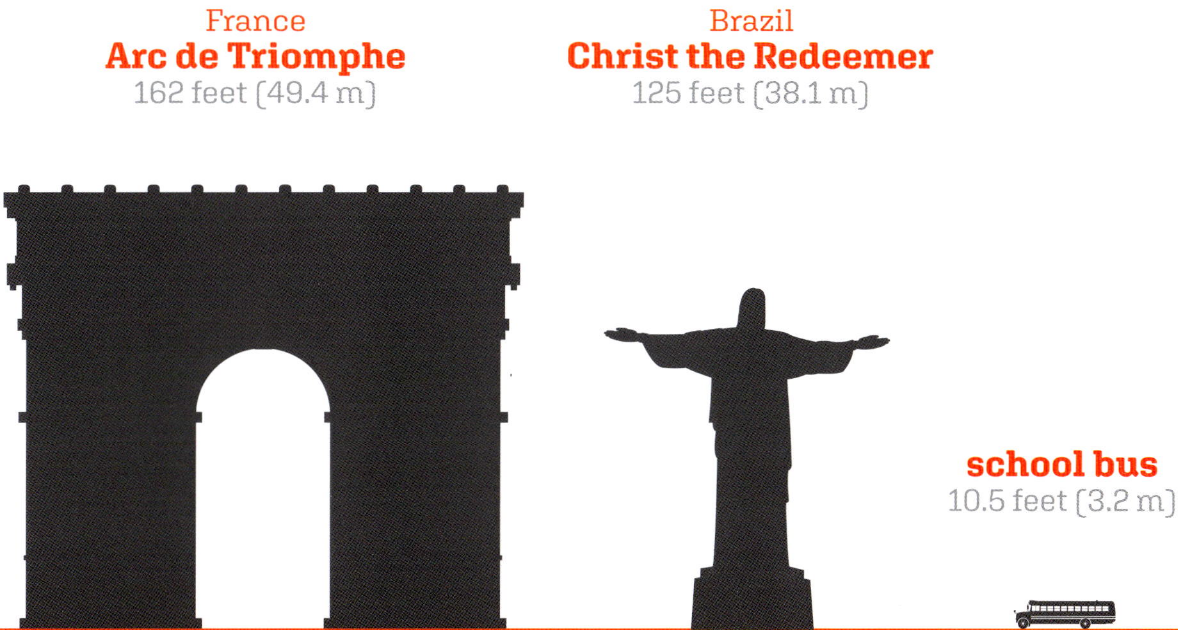

George Washington

George Washington was the nation's first president. People wanted to build something in his honor. Robert Mills designed the monument. A group raised money for it. Construction began on July 4, 1848.

Original design for the Washington Monument

By 1854, it had reached 156 feet (47.5 m). But money ran out. Then the **Civil War** began. Work did not continue for more than 20 years. The monument finally opened to the public in 1888.

◄ **Unfinished Washington Monument (1860)**

555 feet tall

40 years to open

897 steps in its stairway

The Washington Monument is about 555 feet (169 m) tall. At first, workers used large blocks of rock for the **foundation**. Later, they added concrete. They used **pulleys** to lift heavy blocks of marble, granite, and sandstone. The builders did not use **mortar**. Gravity holds the 36,491 blocks together.

◄ Nearly completed Washington Monument

20th 1880.

Early on, a steam-powered elevator carried people to the top. Since then, the elevator has been replaced. After an earthquake in 2011, the building closed for repairs. It has since reopened.

Nearly one million people visit each year. Ride the elevator to the top. On the way, you will see some of the memorial stones inside the monument.

A memorial stone at the 190-foot (57.9 m) landing

Look out the windows in the viewing area. Can you find the Lincoln Memorial? What about the White House? Afterward, explore the National Mall for a closer look at the sites you spotted!

Can you spot these in the picture above?

Lincoln Memorial

U.S. Capitol

Jefferson Memorial

★ Activity ★

Make a Sugar-Cube Monument

materials

sugar cubes

sandpaper

plate

bowl of water

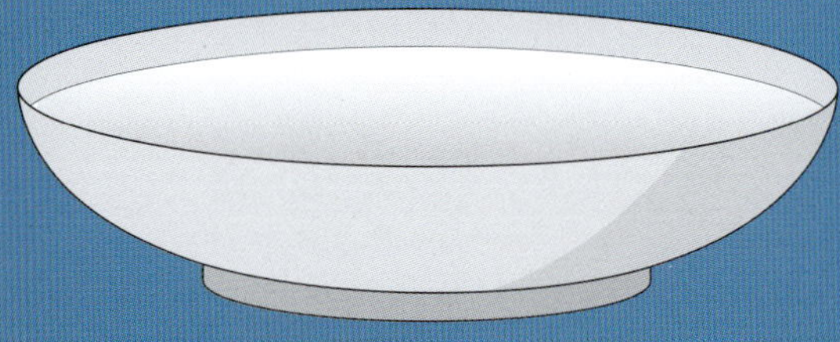

1

Put four cubes in a square on the plate. This is your base layer.

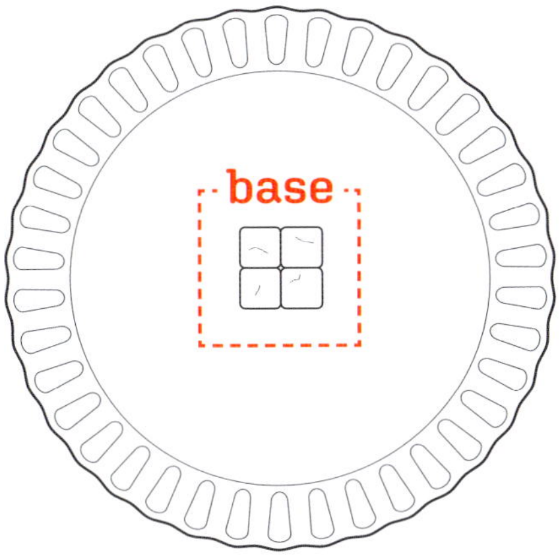

2

Dip sugar cubes in water to help them stick together. Stack more layers on top of the base.

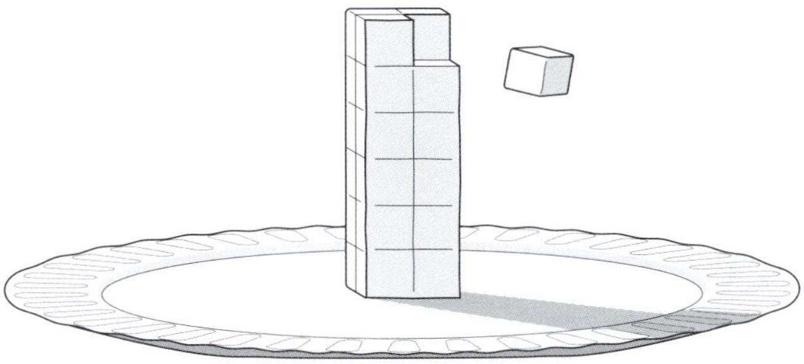

3

Use sandpaper to make the top pyramid. Connect four cubes. Then sand them into a triangle.

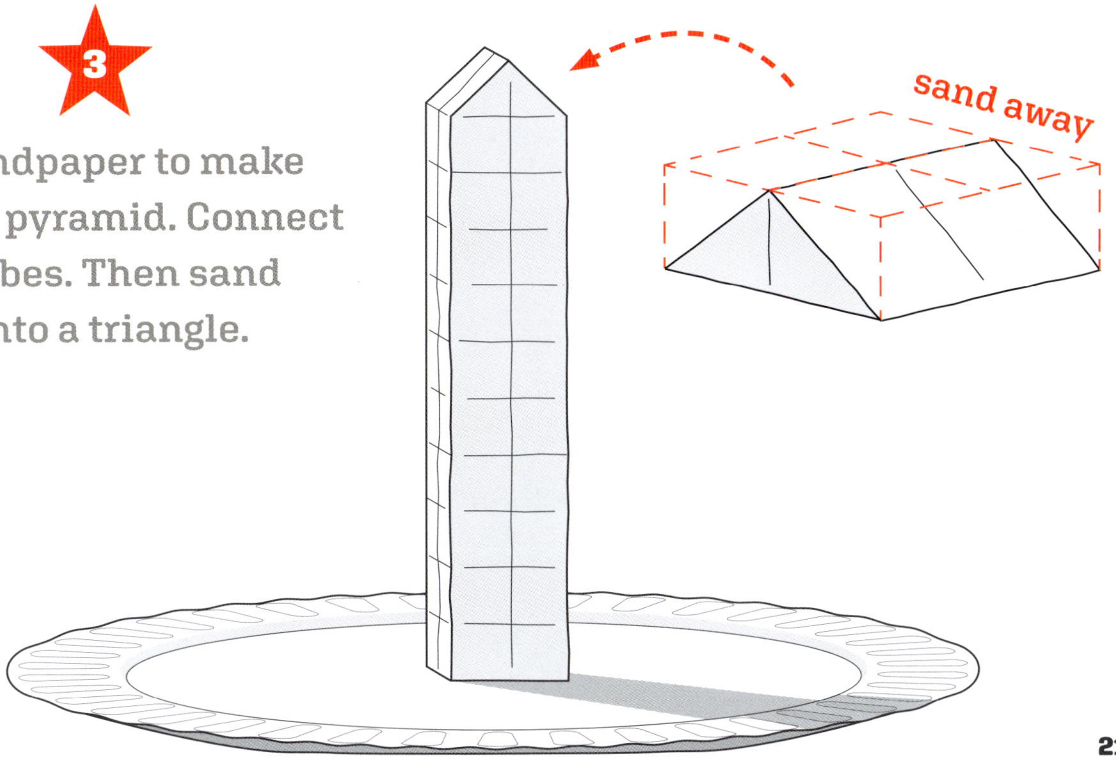

Glossary

Civil War
the war between northern and southern states from 1861 to 1865

foundation
the lowest weight-bearing part of a structure

monument
a structure built to honor a person or event

mortar
a paste used to hold bricks or stones together

pulleys
small wheels with grooved rims around which cords pass

Read More

Hoena, Blake. *Washington, D.C.: The U.S. Capital.* Minneapolis: Bellwether Media, 2014.

Nelson, Kristin L. *The Washington Monument.* Minneapolis: Lerner, 2011.

Websites

National Park Service: Washington Monument

Read more about the monument, and browse a photo gallery.

https://www.nps.gov/wamo/index.htm

PBS: The National Mall - America's Front Yard

Learn more about the history of the Washington Monument.

http://www.pbs.org/program/national-mall-americas-front-yard/

Index

PUBLISHED BY CREATIVE EDUCATION AND CREATIVE PAPERBACKS
P.O. Box 227, Mankato, Minnesota 56002
Creative Education and Creative Paperbacks are imprints of The Creative Company
www.thecreativecompany.us

LIBRARY OF CONGRESS CATALOGING-IN-PUBLICATION DATA
Names: Dittmer, Lori, author.
Title: Washington Monument / Lori Dittmer.
Series: Landmarks of America.
Includes bibliographical references and index.
Summary: Examining the building process from the ground up, this high-interest title covers the history and construction of the Washington Monument, one of Washington, D.C.'s most well-known landmarks.

Identifiers: LCCN: 2018060964
ISBN 978-1-64026-129-7 (hardcover)
ISBN 978-1-62832-692-5 (pbk)
ISBN 978-1-64000-247-0 (eBook)

Subjects: LCSH: Washington Monument (Washington, D.C.)—Juvenile literature. / Washington Monument (Washington, D.C.)—Models. / Washington Monument (Washington, D.C.)—Study and teaching (Elementary)—Activity programs.
Classification: LCC F203.4.W3 D58 2019
DDC 975.3—dc23

DESIGN AND PRODUCTION
by Joe Kahnke; art direction by Rita Marshall
Printed in China

PHOTOGRAPHS by Alamy (The Protected Art Archive), Dreamstime (Joe Sohm), Getty Images (Ken Cedeno/Corbis Historical, Richard Fairless/Moment Open, Library of Congress/Corbis Historical, Universal History Archive/UIG), iStockphoto (Joe_Potato, Pgiam, Tanarch, traveler1116), National Archives and Records Administration (National Archives Identifier: 516531/Department of Agriculture. Bureau of Plant Industry. Office of Horticultural Crops and Diseases. Still Picture Records Section, Special Media Archives Services Division/National Archives at College Park), National Park Service, Shutterstock (BATKA, Orhan Cam, dikobraziy, Dr_Flash, Jellicle, Ingo Menhard, Piotr Przyluski, Alexey Pushkin)

FIRST EDITION HC 9 8 7 6 5 4 3 2 1
FIRST EDITION PBK 9 8 7 6 5 4 3 2 1